Henry and Mudge
IN THE
Green Time

The Third Book of Their Adventures

Story by Cynthia Rylant
Pictures by Suçie Stevenson

BRADBURY PRESS • NEW YORK

For Evan Harper
and his folks — CR

To Helen Languth — SS

THE HENRY AND MUDGE BOOKS

Text copyright © 1987 by Cynthia Rylant
Illustrations copyright © 1987 by Suçie Stevenson
All rights reserved. No part of this book may be reproduced or
transmitted in any form or by any means, electronic or
mechanical, including photocopying, recording or by any
information storage and retrieval system, without permission in
writing from the Publisher.

Bradbury Press
An Affiliate of Macmillan, Inc.
866 Third Avenue, New York, NY 10022
Collier Macmillan Canada, Inc.

Manufactured in the United States of America
10 9 8 7 6 5 4 3 2 1
The text of this book is set in 18 pt. Goudy Old Style.
The illustrations are pen-and-ink and watercolor, reproduced
in full-color.
Book design by Mina Greenstein

Library of Congress Cataloging-in-Publication Data
Rylant, Cynthia. Henry and Mudge in the green time.
Summary: For Henry and his big dog Mudge,
summer means going on a picnic in the park, taking a
bath under the garden hose, and going to the top of
the big green hill.
[1. Dogs—Fiction.   2. Summer—Fiction]
I. Stevenson, Suçie, ill.   II. Title.
PZ7.R982H1   1987   [E]   86-26386
ISBN 0-02-778003-1

Contents

Henry and Mudge

IN THE

Green Time

The Picnic

In the summer,
Henry and his big dog Mudge
liked to go on picnics.

Henry packed the food.
He packed jelly sandwiches,
pears, and gingersnaps
for himself.

He packed dry dog food
and popcorn for Mudge.
They both drank water.

One Sunday they went
to the park for a picnic.
Henry put all the food
on a picnic table,
while Mudge chased some ants
under a tree.

Mudge was so big
that his tail went WHACK!
every time he ran
around the tree.
WHACK! WHACK! WHACK!
WHACK! Henry laughed at him.

Soon they began eating.
Henry chewed his jelly sandwich
while he threw pieces of popcorn
into Mudge's mouth.

Mudge always liked dessert first
on picnics.

While they were eating,
a yellow bee landed on
Henry's pear.
Henry didn't see the bee.
Henry picked up his pear.

"Ow!" Henry cried.

Mudge jumped.

The bee flew away.

"Ow! Ow! Ow!" Henry cried.

He shook his hand again and again
and again.
But his hand hurt more and more.
It hurt a lot.

Tears came to Henry's eyes.
His hand hurt so much.
It had a puffy white
circle on it.

Henry just had to cry.
He sat down beside Mudge
and held on to his hurting hand
and cried.

Mudge sniffed Henry's hair.

Mudge sniffed Henry's hand.

Mudge put his big nose

in Henry's ear.

But Henry kept crying.

Then Mudge licked Henry's face.
Mudge liked the taste.
It was salty.

So Mudge licked Henry's face
again and again and again.

Every tear that Henry cried
Mudge licked away.

Henry cried,

Mudge licked,

and the hand hurt.

But in a while,

the hand stopped hurting,

Henry stopped crying,

and Mudge stopped licking.

Henry looked at Mudge and smiled.

Henry picked up a gingersnap.
He took one bite
and gave Mudge the rest.

"Thanks," said Henry.

Mudge wagged his tail
and waited for another cookie.

The Bath

On hot days Henry liked
to give Mudge a bath.
Henry liked it
because he could
play with the water hose and
because he could cool off.

Mudge hated it.
Mudge knew when
he was going to get
a bath.

He would see Henry
looking for the dog shampoo.

And when he saw Henry hooking up
the water hose,
he tried to hide
under the steps.

But it never worked.

Henry would take Mudge
into the front yard
in the sun, and he would
hose him down.

Mudge hated it.
His eyes drooped,
his ears drooped,
and his tail drooped.

When he was all wet,
he looked like a big walrus.

Henry laughed at him.

Then Henry would soap him up.

Henry scrubbed his head

and his neck

and his back

and his chest

and his stomach

and his legs

and his tail.

Mudge really hated

this part.

He drooped even more.

Then Henry
hosed Mudge down again.

But before Henry
could grab a towel,
before Henry could get Mudge dry,
Mudge always got Henry back.
Because when Henry
let go—

Mudge started shaking.
He started with his head,
then he shook his neck
and his back

and his chest
and his stomach
and his legs
and his tail.

Mudge shook so hard
that when he was done,
he was mostly dry,
and Henry was mostly wet.

Then Mudge looked at Henry
and wagged his tail
while Henry
dried Henry
with the towel.

The Green Time

Beside Henry's house
was a big green hill.
Late on summer days,
Henry and Mudge
went to the top
of the green hill.

They looked down.

They saw Henry's white house.

They saw Henry's blue bike.

They saw Henry's wooden swing.

On top of the green hill,
Henry felt big.

He felt like a king.
He saw his things below
him, and he felt very big.

"I am King of the Green Hill,"
Henry said.

He looked at Mudge.

"You are my dragon."
Mudge wagged his tail.

"Your name," Henry said, "is Fireball."
Mudge wagged again.

"And you are very scary,"
Henry said.
Mudge wagged some more.

Henry and Mudge marched
all over the top
of the green hill.
They met other kings
who had dragons.
They chased them away.

They met monsters.
Mudge ate them.
They marched and marched
till they could
march no more.

Then they found
a magic tree
on the green hill.

It was a tree
for kings and dragons
who were tired.

Henry and Mudge
sat down under the tree.
Henry put his arms
around Mudge.

They were glad
for a magic tree.
They closed their eyes.

And a boy and a dog
slept, together,
on the green hill
in their green time.

19785

19785

E
R

Rylant, Cynthia
Henry and Mudge in the
green time

10.95

DATE DUE	BORROWER'S NAME	
APR 22 '9?	Bernie	
APR 11 '9?	James	
APR 1 8 '9?	Bernice	

Rylant, Cynthia
Henry and Mudge in the
green time